A CHRISTMAS STORY

By Mary Chalmers

Harper & Row, Publishers

For Ursula

It certainly looks as if it is going to snow.

You see? Here is the snow.

"I'm glad we wore our galoshes,"
says Elizabeth to Harry Dog.

Alice Rabbit and Hilary Cat are waiting for them
when they get home.
"We found a lovely tree," says Elizabeth.

Alice and Hilary have made some hot chocolate.
They all sit down and have some.

Then they bring the Christmas tree decorations
down from the attic.

They get right to work.
It is a big job to trim the tree,
and, you know,
it isn't every little girl
and dog and cat and rabbit
who can do it.

"Ohhhhhhh!

They work hard.

Hilary decides to taste the popcorn string.
"Hilary, you stop that," says Elizabeth.

The tree is all trimmed.
But there is no star for the top.

"I'll go get one," says Elizabeth.

Elizabeth meets a lady.
The lady doesn't have a star,
but she has a ginger cookie for her.

Elizabeth becomes a little lost in the woods,
but a blue jay shows her the way out.
He doesn't have a star, though.

Elizabeth passes a dark cave.
"Hello! Is anyone there?" she calls.
One pair of eyes opens,
and then two and three, four,
five pairs of eyes.
Five owls in there.
"Do you have a star for me?" asks Elizabeth.
"No, no star here," say the five owls.
They aren't interested in stars
for the tops of Christmas trees just now.
They are too sleepy.

What luck!
Elizabeth meets the Santa Claus
for rabbits and other small animals.
"Do you know," says Elizabeth,
"we don't have a star
for the top of our Christmas tree."

"Well, now, let's see," says the Santa Claus.
"There just might be one in here somewhere."

"Ho, ho!" he says. "Here we are!"

There!